W9-ACH-318

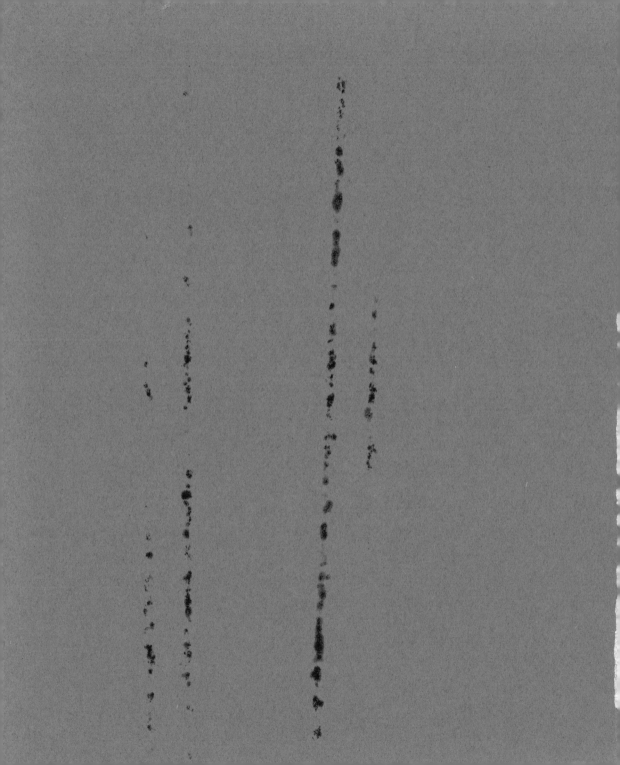

Illustrated by **nance studio**

The Whang Doodle

Folk Tales
from the Carolinas

edited by JEAN COTHRAN

sandlapper press, inc.

For LISA, KENNY, RUSH, MARY, POLLY, and SASHA

FIRST EDITION

Copyright © 1972 by SANDLAPPER PRESS, INC.

International Standard Book Number: 0-87844-016-X
Library of Congress Catalog Card Number: LC-72-86904

Published by Sandlapper Press, Inc., P.O. Box 1668,
Columbia, S.C. 29202

CONTENTS

ADDIE'S PLAT-EYE   1

PAPPY'S TATER PATCH   5

THE WHANG DOODLE   11

HOW THE RABBIT STOLE THE OTTER'S COAT   18

WHY THE POSSUM'S TAIL IS BARE   22

THE TALKING MULE   25

THE BALL GAME OF THE BIRDS AND THE ANIMALS   28

THE SPIDER HELPER   32

ROOSTER IN THE TREE   35

A HOP-TOAD IN A GOURD   38

THE ENCHANTED CLOAK   41

WHO STOLE BUH KINLAW'S GOAT?   45

THE RABBIT, FOX AND GOOSE   48

BETSEY LONG-TOOTH   54

CINDUH SEED IN YOU POCKET   60

HOW THE DEER GOT HIS HORNS   64

A LOAD OF WATERMELON   67

DING, A-DING, DING   70

BUDDAH RABBIT AND THE MUSIC MAN   73

THE TAILFISHER   77

SEVEN BLUE BUTTERFLIES   79

ABOUT THE TALES   86

ACKNOWLEDGMENTS   89

ADDIE'S PLAT-EYE

There's Addie—her face a web of wrinkles, her hair plaited down and tightly wrapped with white twine. Her clothes hang on her spare frame like a scarecrow, but she's busy bringing up her great-grands. In her yard the crepe myrtle blooms, red birds visit, sunflowers turn their faces east. Green corn waves behind her shack. Wild plum trees hang heavy and a bantam rooster struts and crows.

1

"Plat-eye? Yas'm," says Addie. "The old folks talk about plat-eye. They say they takes the shape of all kinds of critter—dog, cat, hog, mule, varmint—and I even hear tell of plat-eye taking form of 'gator."

But Addie only saw a plat-eye once. She'd been digging for clams and the tide had come in very late in the evening. Going home it was dusky dark when she hit Parsonage Lane and passed the Captain's barn and stable. She wasn't afraid at all. She had her bloom on her in those days. They were milking at the barn, and she said, "Good eben, Cap'n Bill!" And he gave her back her word.

Soon she was passing the graveyard entrance. She left the open and entered the dark woods, where the moss hung low and brushed her face. Then she began to think about plat-eye. The mind came to her it was a good time to meet them. She pushed the weeping moss aside and traveled the wet mud in her bare feet, with her shoes tied to her girdle string. And when she came to the foot log, she saw that same old cypress that's there now (It blew down in the last big September gale). Mr. Bull Frog hit the water—kerplunk. A cooter [turtle] slid off the log at her feet.

Then she turned her eyes up and there was a cat. A black cat with eyes like balls of fire and his back all arched up, his tail twisting and switching and his hair on end. He backed in front of her 'cross that cypress log. He was big as her little yearling ox, and she said to him, "I ain't fer fear nuttin'. Ain't no ghost! Ain't no hant! Ain't no plat-eye! Ain't no nuttin'!"

She tried to sing a hymn, but the plat-eye moved forward, swishing his tail like a big moccasin lashing the rushes. Then she braced up. Her short-handled clam rake was in her hand and the mind came to her, "De Lawd heps dem what heps deyse'f."

2

Addie raised up her rake and came down right across that critter's head. If he had been a real cat, she'd have pinned him to the log. But that cat pranced right up under her feet, his eyes burning holes in her. She struggled to get her rake loose from the log, and then came down straight through the critter's middle, but he didn't even feel her lick.

"No, man!" Addie recalls. "Mr. Plat-eye just as pert and frisky as 'fore he bin hit. And I 'buse [abuse] 'em and I cuss 'em and I say, 'You debbil! Clear my path!' "

But the critter pawed the air and went up a big bamboo vine, so her mind came to her to travel the woods path. She turned to make haste and hit the path. She was just giving the Lord the praise for delivering her when there was that cat again. This time he was big as her middle-size ox and his eyes were ablaze. And she lam and lam, and just as she made her last lam that critter rose up before her eyes and this time he was big as Cousin Andrew's full-grown ox. He vanished up that old boxed pine just as you quit the deep woods.

Addie didn't believe in plat-eye until then, but she watches her steps since that day. When she travels the deep woods where the moss is low and Mr. Cooter lives and Mr. Moccasin crawls and Firefly flickers, her pocket is loaded.

"Yas'm," says Addie, "I's ready fer 'em." Uncle Murphy, the witch doctor, told her how to fend them off, and they haven't troubled her again. Gun powder and sulphur mixed. Plat-eye can't stand the smell.

"So," says Addie, "I totes my powder and sulphur and carries my stick in my hand, and I puts my trust in the Lord."

4

PAPPY'S TATER PATCH

My pappy was the farmin'est feller what ever lived. He raised a big family of young'uns and it took a lot of scrambling to keep us all fed. Our land was rough, all 'cept a little patch of bottom, and we kept the bottom farmed to death.

Behind the house was a little knob that was durn nigh straight up into the air. It was all covered with thicket and rocks and warn't fit

5

for nothing but hoot owls and snakes. Looked just like a monster funnel turned upside down.

As us young'uns got bigger and got to eating heartier, Pappy began to worry about how he could feed us all. Fin'ly he told us at supper one night that he was aiming to clear the knob and plant it with taters. Now Pappy never stood for no funny business, but we young'uns and Ma couldn't help from laughing at him, axing him did he mean to burn out the brush and shoot in the seed taters with his shotgun. All he had to say back was that we'd start clearing the knob come morning.

He got us all started grubbing and toting rocks offen the knob. I'll swear, that knob was so steep we'd dig in with our toes, and when we'd slip there was no stopping till we hit the bottom. Ever one of us was all skinned and bruised up by night. But Pappy held us to it for about a week, and at last we had that old knob skinned clean as a peeled onion.

Then Pappy throwed a rope over his shoulder, took the axe and a big stake, and inched his way to the top. At the very top he drove in the stake, good and solid. He tied one end of the rope to the stake and slid down, bringing the other end back to the bottom. Then he hitched the old mule to the plow, brought her up to the foot of the knob, and tied the loose end of the rope around the mule. Pappy got a good holt on the handles of the plow, geehawed the old mule, and started plowing a furrow at the bottom of the knob. As the mule went round, the upper end of the rope wrapped 'round the stake, and that worked the mule and the plow and Pappy up the knob. Pappy had to lean over until his right ear 'most touched the ground, and the right-handed pocket of his jeans scooped up dirt.

Well, Pappy fin'ly got the knob plowed up. Then he got us

young'uns together, filled our pockets with tater eyes, and each one of us picked out a row and started snaking along on our bellies, planting them tater eyes. The first night it rained, and all the tater eyes washed out to the foot of the knob. Next day we did it all over. Fin'ly they took root and began to grow.

When them taters was high enough to cultivate, we wondered how Pappy would get 'em hoed. We weren't long in finding out. Pappy got out his rope again, tied one end to the stake on top of the knob, and tied a knot in the britches belt of each of us young'uns and started us hoeing. We were strung out up that durn knob like a maypole dance, but it worked and we got the taters hoed.

That was the richest ground I ever heard tell of. When the taters started growing, humps were pushed up all over the knob like as if the knob had been stung by a million big hornets. Pappy was so proud of that tater patch he didn't pay no mind to the rest of the place at all.

When it came time to harvest the taters, we all got baskets and towbags and Pappy hitched up the old mule to the plow and started plowing out the bottom row. The taters had growed so close together that they was resting on each other. When the bottom row came out, it was like knocking the end gate outen a load of sand. Them taters just started rolling down the knob like a landslide, and there was the durndest rumbling and roaring I ever heard. Pappy let out a yell, unhitched the mule, and hollered: "Ever' man for hisself!" We all took to the tall timber until the tater slide was over.

Them taters covered the ground all 'round the house ten feet deep. We had to dig a tunnel to the house and outbuildings. Ever'thing was buried 'neath taters. We worked all the rest of the fall and winter carting them taters to market.

We made enough money to buy a farm in the valley, and we all worked on Pappy to move so's we young'uns could get to school. He wouldn't hear to leaving. He sent Ma and us young'uns to the valley, and gave us money, but he never would move away from that wonderful tater patch.

Pappy would come to see us 'casionally, and he got so he leaned way over on the right side when he walked, and I noticed that his right ear always was dirty and his right-hand jeans pocket always had dirt in it. Ever' fall about the same time we'd hear a rumbling from the direction of the mountain farm, and we knowed that Pappy was harvesting his taters.

THE WHANG DOODLE

Until I was a growed-up man I'd kite out like a rabbit in the tall grass if anybody so much as mentioned a Whang Doodle in my hearin'. Even now, when a body says anythin' 'bout one of them critters, my skin begins to crinkle up and seems like I cain't keep my eyeballs from rollin'.

I ain't sayin' I ever met a Whang Doodle face to face, and I don't know as I can tell 'zactly what one looks like, but I come up on one of the varmints oncet, and that's enough for me. All I seed was a big flash of gray fur and a pair of green eyes with lightnin' in 'em, makin' the awfulest yowl I ever heered—but that's gettin' ahead some, I rekon.

I was jes' a shirt-tail boy, this winter I'm tellin' 'bout, and I had toted in a pile of lightwood, and the chimbley jamb was heaped with logs what me and Pappy'd cut in the afternoon. It seem nice and cozy 'round the blazin' hearth, and I's thinkin' to myself, a boy's lucky what's got a good pappy and a good mammy, and a little kid brother, and good rations to eat, and a place to sleep, and a nice fire on a cold night.

Sure seem nice! Pappy was a-settin' afore the fire borin' out corncobs and fixin' hisself some new pipes. Mammy was a-burnin' a hole through the pith of some fig stems with a red-hot darnin' needle for the pipe stems. Smelt powerful good, them burnin' fig stems! Ever oncet in a while Mammy'd stoop over and heat the needle in the embers. First the needle'd be black; then when Mammy fotches it outen the fire it's red-hot and glowin'.

Pappy look over at Mammy, and he grin and say, "That-air needle look jes' like the Whang Doodle's tongue; dog ef it don't."

Mammy she look up quick and say, "What you tryin' to do—skeer these chillun into fits with you' brash talk 'bout that varmint? Better be puttin' you' thoughts 'longside with the Good Book and talkin' that kinda talk, 'stead such foolishment as you talkin' now." She jerked the needle outen the fire, and when it was cool she lay it on the fireboard. She still a-scowlin' at Pappy, but he not worried much 'bout Mammy's scoldin'. He jes' rare back in his chair and he shet his eyes tight and he sing:

12

Whang Doodle holler, and Whang Doodle squall,
Look out, chillun, do he git you all.

Mammy she stop what she a-doin', and she say, "I bet iffen you don't shet you' mouth like I done tole you, I'se gwine to up and bash you a good'un with this yere long-handle spider" [a legged pan to cook over embers].

Pappy sort of settle down atter that. He know not to rile Mammy too fur, do she bash him one sure 'nuff, like she say she will. Mammy she say, "Time you chillun git off to bed, anyhow. Moe, you git me them cardin' boards and lemme give you all's hair a good combin'. You sure a passel of nappy haids." When Mammy gits through with Jim Baby and come my time, seem like she goin' right down to my brains. Then she say, "Yo'll wash you' foots, and mind you washes 'em good, and git on off to bed."

Me and Jim Baby sleeps in the shed room where Mammy keeps her strings of leather britches [drying string beans] and hot peppers. They was hung from the rafters, and the light shinin' in from the hearth makes big shadders on the wall, a-jigglin' and a-jumpin' like spooks and hants. Jim Baby wake up and see them shadders a-trapsin' on the wall, and he grob me and say, "Moe, you reckon that's the ole Whang Doodle a-dancin'?"

And I say, "Jim boy, no, them's not the Whang Doodle, them's jes' shadders on the wall."

Long atter us chilluns is in bed, I's layin' awake. Seem like I jes' cain't git to sleep, thinkin' 'bout the ole Whang Doodle what Pappy done tole 'bout. I 'members what Pete Bunker say,

13

The Whang Doodle moaneth
And the Doodle Bug whineth,

and I feels the goose bumps jes' risin'. I slides over clost to Jim Baby, 'cause I's skeered. He holler in his sleep, "Look out, Moe, how you scrougin' me. I's sleepy and wants you to leave me be."

I lay there, as I say, a long time, thinkin' 'bout that critter whut nobody cain't see. Pappy and Mammy is a-snorin' in they bed, and it was so quiet you can hear the mice a-squeakin' and ole Dan a-scratchin' fleas under the house. It was jes' one of them black-dark nights, and I keep a-wishin' I can go to sleep so's I can forgit how skeered I is.

All to oncet, out of the quiet and seem like way off, I hears a long scream: "Ye-e-e-ow-ow-ow."

I jumps right outen the bed, and helt my breaf, and say, "Dear Lawd, look atter me and mine."

Nothin' don't happen for a spell. Ever'thing is still and quiet. Ole Dan quits a-scratchin' his fleas and the mice quit a-runnin' round. Then, seem like right down by the hawg lot, come that scream agin.

You never heered sech a scatterment in all you' born days. I shakes and trembles. I thinks I shorely die. Pappy he wake up and go lookin' for his goose gun. Mammy she wake up and gits the lantern lit.

The hawgs is a-screamin' fitten to kill, and Pappy yell to me, "Moe, you git up and hustle. Somethin' is a-gittin' the hawgs."

Iffen I'd a-had my way, I'd snuggle down in the bed and pull the kivers over my haid. I know iffen I don't come out, Pappy come in there and jerk me out, so I pulls on my pants, and foller him, so trembly I cain't hardly stand on my laigs.

16   Pappy he goes ahead with the gun, and Mammy she follers with the

lantern, holdin' it up high. I come behind Mammy, holdin' to the battlin' board, but I reckon I couldn't hit a flea with it, I's shakin' so bad. Time we gits down the path a piece here comes Jim Baby, cryin' and hollerin', "Wait for me, wait for me—I's skeered." He brung up the rear.

We cropt, single file, 'round the wash house, 'round the spring house, past the branch, and to'rds the hawg pen. The hawgs is a-carryin' on somethin' terrible, screamin' like's if all they throats is bein' cut.

Jes' then the light from Mammy's lantern ketched the varmint's eyeballs, and I see them big balls of green fire inside the hawg pen. Pappy raises up the ole gun and fires, and it sounds like the roar of the heavenly cannon. The old gun kick Pappy, and he tumbles back on Mammy. Mammy she drap the lantern and falls down, and seem like my laigs jes' fold up and I's a-layin' on the ground, too. Jim Baby he takes to his heels and lights out fer the house, yellerin' and bawlin' hard as he can.

That ole critter skins over the fence of the hawg pen, and I catches a glimpse of him. He looks like he as long as a cow, as high as a goat, and got big ears like a mule. He look like a pinter [panther] but he ain't no pinter. He all gray, and woolly. He take one big jump to'rds the woods, and he lets out his yell: "Ye-e-e-ow-ow-ow."

Pappy gits to his foots and grobs me by the scruff of the neck and he say, "Boy, run fer the house. Yonder goes the Whang Doodle."

Mammy ran, and Pappy ran, and I ran, and we gits in the house, all out of breaf, and Jim Baby he already in there, hidin' in the bed with all the kivers pulled up over him. Pappy pulls the door shet and bolts it tight.

Man, I don't never want to see no more Whang Doodle, no suh, ne-ver.

HOW THE RABBIT STOLE THE OTTER'S COAT

The animals were of different sizes and wore coats of various colors and patterns. Some wore long fur and others wore short. Some had rings on their tails, and some had no tails at all. Some had coats of brown, others of black or yellow. They were always disputing about their good looks, so at last they agreed to hold a council to decide who had the finest coat.

18

They had heard a great deal about the Otter, who lived so far up the creek that he seldom came down to visit the other animals. It was said that he had the finest coat of all, but no one knew just what it was like, because it was a long time since anyone had seen him. They did not even know exactly where he lived—only the general direction; but they knew he would come to the council when the word got out.

Now the Rabbit wanted the verdict for himself, so when it began to look as if it might go to the Otter he studied up a plan to cheat him out of it. He asked a few sly questions until he learned what trail the Otter would take to get to the council place. Then, without saying anything, he went on ahead and after four days' travel he met the Otter and knew him at once by his beautiful coat of soft dark-brown fur. The Otter was glad to see him and asked him where he was going. "Oh," said the Rabbit, "the animals sent me to bring you to the council, because you live so far away they were afraid you mightn't know the road." The Otter thanked him, and they went on together.

They traveled all day toward the council ground, and at night the Rabbit selected the camping place, because the Otter was a stranger in that part of the country, and cut down bushes for beds and fixed everything in good shape. The next morning they started on again. In the afternoon the Rabbit began to pick up wood and bark as they went along and to load it on his back. When the Otter asked what this was for, the Rabbit said it was that they might be warm and comfortable at night. After a while, when it was near sunset, they stopped and made their camp.

When supper was over the Rabbit got a stick and shaved it down to a paddle. The Otter wondered and asked again what that was for.

"I have good dreams when I sleep with a paddle under my head," said the Rabbit.

When the paddle was finished the Rabbit began to cut away the bushes so as to make a clean trail down to the river. The Otter wondered more and more and wanted to know what this meant.

Said the Rabbit, "This place is called Di'tatlaski'yi [The Place Where it Rains Fire]. Sometimes it rains fire here, and the sky looks a little that way tonight. You go to sleep and I'll sit up and watch, and if the fire does come, as soon as you hear me shout, you run and jump into the river. Better hang your coat on a limb over there, so it won't get burnt."

The Otter did as he was told, and they both doubled up to go to sleep, but the Rabbit kept awake. After a while the fire burned down to red coals. The Rabbit called, but the Otter was fast asleep and made no answer. In a little while he called again, but the Otter never stirred. Then the Rabbit filled the paddle with hot coals and threw them up into the air and shouted, "It's raining fire! It's raining fire!"

The hot coals fell all around the Otter and he jumped up. "To the water!" cried the Rabbit, and the Otter ran and jumped into the river, and he has lived in the water ever since.

The Rabbit took the Otter's coat and put it on, leaving his own instead, and went on to the council. All the animals were there, every one looking out for the Otter. At last they saw him in the distance, and they said one to the other, "The Otter is coming!" and sent one of the small animals to show him the best seat. They were all glad to see him and went up in turn to welcome him, but the Otter kept his head down, with one paw over his face. They wondered that he was so bashful, until the Bear came up and pulled the paw away, and there was the Rabbit with his split nose.

He sprang up and started to run, when the Bear struck at him and pulled his tail off, but the Rabbit was too quick for them and got away.

WHY THE POSSUM'S TAIL IS BARE

The Possum used to have a long, bushy tail, and was so proud of it that he combed it out every morning and sang about it at the dance, until the Rabbit, who had had no tail since the Bear pulled it out, became very jealous and made up his mind to play the Possum a trick.

There was to be a great council and a dance at which all the

animals were to be present. It was the Rabbit's business to send out the news, so as he was passing the Possum's place he stopped to ask him if he intended to be there. The Possum said he would come if he could have a special seat, "because I have such a handsome tail that I ought to sit where everybody can see me." The Rabbit promised to attend to it and to send someone besides to comb and dress the Possum's tail for the dance, so the Possum was very much pleased and agreed to come.

Then the Rabbit went over to the Cricket, who is such an expert hair cutter that the Indians call him the barber, and told him to go next morning and dress the Possum's tail for the dance that night. He told the Cricket just what to do and then went on about some other mischief.

In the morning the Cricket went to the Possum's house and said he had come to get him ready for the dance. So the Possum stretched himself out and shut his eyes while the Cricket combed out his tail and wrapped a red string around it to keep it smooth until night. But all this time, as he wound the string around, he was clipping off the hair close to the roots, and the Possum never knew it.

When it was night the Possum went to the townhouse where the dance was to be and found the best seat ready for him, just as the Rabbit had promised. When his turn came in the dance he loosened the string from his tail and stepped into the middle of the floor. The drummers began to drum and the Possum began to sing, "See my beautiful tail." Everybody shouted and he danced around the circle and sang again, "See what a fine color it has." They shouted again and he danced around another time, singing, "See how it sweeps the ground." The animals shouted more loudly than ever, and the Possum was delighted. He danced around again and sang, "See how fine the fur is." Then everybody laughed so long that the Possum wondered what they meant. He looked around the circle of animals and they were all laughing at him. Then he looked down at his beautiful tail and saw that there was not a hair left upon it, but that it was as bare as the tail of a lizard. He was so much astonished and ashamed that he could not say a word, but rolled over helpless on the ground and grinned, as the Possum does to this day when taken by surprise.

THE TALKING MULE

Once a man had a mule. And the mule was named Jack. Every Sunday morning the man would send his boy down to the stable to get the mule and plough all day.

One more Sunday the man sent the boy to the stable and, as always, he said, "Stand back, Jack!"

So this Sunday morning when the boy went in the stable and said,

"Stand back, Jack," to his surprise the mule gave him an answer.

"Every Sunday morning it's 'Stand back, Jack; stand back, Jack,' " said the mule.

The boy was scared. He ran back and told his poppa, "The mule's talking."

"No, he isn't! Go hitch up."

"You come and see," said the boy.

When the man got there, the mule was still saying, "Every Sunday morning, it's 'Stand back, Jack!' "

26

The old man was scared. He started to run. As he ran, he hollered, "I never heard that mule talk in my life before!" He kept running and hollering, "I never heard a mule talk!"

The man had a little dog. Little dog, right behind him, said, "Me neither."

Every time the man said, "I never heard a mule talk," little dog said, "Me neither."

That was the last time that mule was ever hitched up on a Sunday.

THE BALL GAME OF THE
BIRDS AND THE ANIMALS

Once the animals challenged the birds to a great ballplay, and the birds accepted. The leaders made the arrangements and fixed the day, and when the time came both parties met at the place for the ball dance, the animals on a smooth grassy bottom near the river and the birds in the treetops over by the ridge. The captain of the animals was the Bear, who was so strong and heavy that he could pull down anyone who got in his way. All along the road to the ball ground he was tossing up great logs to show his strength and boasting of what he would do to the birds when the game began. The Terrapin, too—not the one we have now, but the great original Terrapin—was with the animals. His shell was so hard that the heaviest blows could not hurt him, and he kept rising up on his hind legs and dropping heavily again to the ground, bragging that this was the way he would crush any bird that tried to take the ball from him. Then there was the Deer, who could outrun every other animal. Altogether it was a fine company.

The birds had the Eagle for their captain, with the Hawk and the great *Tla'nuwa,* all swift and strong of flight, but still they were a little afraid of the animals. The dance was over and they were all pruning their feathers up in the trees and waiting for the captain to give the word when here came two little things hardly larger than field mice climbing up the tree in which sat perched the bird captain. At last they reached the top, and creeping along the limb to where the Eagle captain sat they asked to be allowed to join in the game. The captain looked at them, and seeing that they were four-footed, he asked why they did not go to the animals, where they belonged. The little things said that they had, but the animals had made fun of them and driven them off because they were so small. Then the bird captain pitied them and wanted to take them.

But how could they join the birds when they had no wings? The Eagle, the Hawk, and the others consulted, and at last it was decided to make some wings for the little fellows. They tried for a long time to think of something that might do, until someone happened to remember the drum they had used in the dance. The head was of ground-hog skin and maybe they could cut off a corner and make

29

wings of it. So they took two pieces of leather from the drumhead and cut them into shape for wings, and stretched them with cane splints and fastened them on to the forelegs of one of the small animals, and in this way came *Tla'meha,* the Bat. They threw the ball to him and told him to catch it, and by the way he dodged and circled about, keeping the ball always in the air and never letting it fall to the ground, the birds soon saw that he would be one of their best men.

Now they wanted to fix the other little animal, but they had used up all their leather to make wings for the Bat, and there was no time to send for more. Somebody said that they might do it by stretching his skin, so two large birds took hold from opposite sides with their strong bills, and by pulling at his fur for several minutes they managed to stretch the skin on each side between the fore and hind feet, until they had *Tewa,* the Flying Squirrel. To try him the bird captain threw up the ball, then the Flying Squirrel sprang off the limb after it, caught it in his teeth and carried it through the air to another tree nearly across the bottom.

When they were all ready the signal was given and the game began, but almost at the first toss the Flying Squirrel caught the ball and carried it up a tree, from which he threw it to the birds, who kept it in the air for some time until it dropped. The Bear rushed to get it, but the Martin darted after it and threw it to the Bat, who was flying near the ground, and by his dodging and doubling kept it out of the way of even the Deer, until he finally threw it in between the posts and won the game for the birds.

The Bear and the Terrapin, who had boasted so of what they would do, never got a chance even to touch the ball. For saving the ball when it dropped, the birds afterwards gave the Martin a gourd in which to build his nest, and he still has it.

A SPIDER HELPER

Once there was a very mischievous Indian boy. His mother tried to look after him because his father was dead.

After one of his escapades, the white men who lived close by the tribe's territory chased him for his life. All night they followed him but the boy kept ahead of his pursuers. His mother, greatly worried about her son, knelt down beneath the waxing moon and asked the Great Spirit to take care of him.

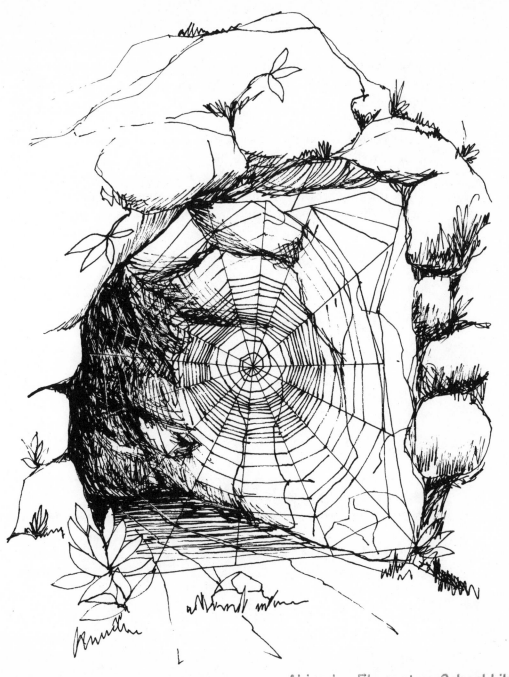

At first light the boy hid in a cave by a rock cliff. After he had gone into the hole, a spider began to weave its web across the opening. Back and forth it went until its threads covered the entrance.

The enemy tracked the boy to the cave but when they saw the spider's web across the entrance they stopped, thinking no one could be inside. Off they went another way and finally gave up their chase. When the boy returned to his tribe, his mother was grateful for his escape. The Great Spirit, said the old Indian woman, had answered her prayer.

ROOSTER IN THE TREE

The rooster was scratching under a tree when his old enemy, the fox, came along. The rooster quickly flew up in the tree to get out of his way.

"Come on down," said the tricky old fox. "Don't be scared of me. I won't hurt you. Don't you know peace has been declared between the birds of the air and the animals of the ground?"

"No," said the rooster. "I didn't know of it."

"Well it's a fact," said the fox. "Word has gone round and everybody has heard the good news."

Just then from where the rooster was sitting way up in the tree he could see some dogs coming over the hill, sniffing the fox's trail.

Said the rooster, "Well, if that's true, I'll be down directly. I see some dogs coming over the hill to join us."

Before the words were out of the rooster's mouth, the deceitful fox was long gone from the foot of the tree.

A HOP-TOAD IN A GOURD

 Once there was a man and his son who knew very little about the animals who shared their woods. They didn't even know a terrapin. One day when they were chopping trees, they came upon a highland terrapin. The animal was frightened and quickly drew in its head and closed up its shell.

"Look here, what's that thing?" said the boy.

"Don't know," answered the father, "I never saw anything that could swallow its own head before."

When they'd finished cutting their trees, they went to see a man they thought knew more than they did.

Said the man who was supposed to be wiser, "You must have seen a hop-toad in a gourd."

THE ENCHANTED CLOAK

There was once in this town a young girl who so desired the love of a certain young man that she took all the money she possessed and bought a handsome cloak, with the beauty of which she might attract him and win his love.

The young man, however, being thrifty, and having heard it said that a woman may throw out of a window with a spoon more money than a man can throw in at the door with a shovel, was so put out by her extravagance that, instead of being charmed by the beauty of the cloak, he was so offended by her thriftlessness that he quarrelled with her, left her, and did not come back; so that she never saw him again.

She was heartbroken; and, loving him desperately, she pined away and died. On her deathbed, perceiving that the cloak had been the cause of all her sorrow, she cursed it with a bitter curse.

After her death the cloak was sold to a second-hand-clothes dealer. It was still a rich and handsome garment, and bore upon it no trace of her misfortune or her tears.

There were also in this town two young girls, both so pretty and so charming that it was difficult for a lover to choose between them.

These two girls were sworn friends for life; neither one could exist without the other. But both were in love with the same young man, who, apparently, was indifferently pleased with either.

Now, women may be devoted friends; but when love comes in, a woman will serve her own desire. So, to end the matter, the first young girl took all the money she possessed and bought a beautiful cloak from the second-hand-clothes dealer, with which to please her lover.

But the first time she wore it, hoping to please him, the young man was seized with such an aversion to her that he left her and would not come back.

Her heart was well-nigh broken, seeing that she had gone the wrong way to please him. She thought bitterly on her unexpected misfortune. Her thoughts troubled her so much that she could not sleep, but lay awake all night studying her trouble.

Morning was long in coming. But when it came she had

comprehended the reason of her misfortune—the too handsome cloak without a doubt was the source and cause of her bad luck. Morning brought wisdom also. Perceiving that the cloak had been the cause of her misfortune, and that it was laden with trouble for its owner, and being a generous girl as well as a smart one, she gave the cloak to her bosom friend—as a mark of her undying affection.

WHO STOLE BUH KINLAW'S GOAT?

Once upon a time de cat drink wine,
De monkey chaw tobacco on de street-car line.

There was a man named Buh Kinlaw. Buh Rabbit stole Buh
Kinlaw's goat, and Buh Kinlaw was going to court to find out who
robbed him. So Buh Rabbit saw Buh Woof and said, "Buh Wolf,
deh's t'irty dollahs on a song, t'irty dollahs on a song. Big time on

45

court day. You bass me on de song an' we make a heap o' money. Now when I sing,

'Buh Wof t'ief Buh Kinlaw goat,'

you sing,

'Yes, indeed, indeed I did.',"

So Buh Wolf agreed, and they tried out the song until they could sing it well.

When court day came, Buh Rabbit and Buh Wolf came to town. When they came close to the court place, Buh Rabbit said, "All right, Buh Wolf, time to start singing." And he began,

"Buh Wolf t'ief Buh Kinlaw goat,"

and Buh Wolf came in strong on, "Yes, indeed, indeed I did."

So the judge heard them and said, "So dat's de man what stole Buh Kinlaw goat." And he gave Buh Wolf thirty days instead of thirty dollars.

THE RABBIT, FOX
AND GOOSE

What start the thing off? There was a man who had a garden of vegetables and a little girl. The little girl stayed home, but the father always went to work.

Now Buddah Rabbit was tricky and cunning, so he came to the garden and called, "Lil gal! Oh lil gal!"

The little girl said, "Suh?"

Buddah Rabbit told her, "Your father said turn me in the garden at twelve o'clock; turn me out at one."

"Aw right, suh."

So the little girl turned him in at twelve o'clock, and when one o'clock came she turned him out.

And next day, same thing again. Buddah Rabbit came, "Lil gal, ole man said turn me in one o'clock, and turn me out at two."

Day after, the little girl let him in at two, turned him out at three. Day after that, Buddah Rabbit right back. He did like that man's vegetables. "Lil gal, lil gal!"

"Suh?"

"Ole man say let me in at t'ree; turn me out at four."

This time old man, coming home, happened to go in the garden. Fine vegetables and stuff all cropped down—bit off. Garden ruined. He said, "Who crop up de garden, ruin um all lak dis?"

The little girl said, "Daddy, Buddah Rabbit come. He say you say turn him in twelve o'clock an' turn him out one; turn him in one o'clock an' turn him out two; turn him in two o'clock an' turn him out t'ree!"

Her daddy said, "I tell you what do. When Buddah Rabbit come agin, turn him in but don't turn him out."

Next day Buddah Rabbit came, called out, "Lil gal, lil gal!"

The little girl turned him in. Buddah Rabbit ate and ate. He ate and ate. Four o'clock came and he wanted to get out. He squinched up by the gate and called out, "Lil gal, ain't it four o'clock yet?"

Little girl said she'd got to bake some biscuit and Buddah Rabbit could wait a while. She'd tell him when it was time to turn out.

Buddah Rabbit said, "Gracious! Take a long time for four o'clock come."

"No, Buddah Rabbit. Daddy say when you come dis time, mustn't turn you out till he come."

And Buddah Rabbit went to begging, "Oh do please, lil gal, turn me out! Please, lil gal! Do please, lil gal!"

But she didn't turn him out. Old man, he came home. He came home and Buddah Rabbit still in the garden. Buddah Rabbit squinch up by the gate so when the man open gate he can slip out.

Man didn't open the door but a crack, and he slipped in. He saw Buddah Rabbit squinch up by the gate jam.

"Hey Buddah Rabbit, what you doin' in there?"

Buddah Rabbit said nothing.

"What you doin' in there, Buddah Rabbit?"

Buddah Rabbit said nothing.

The man said, "I believe I kill you! But you too poor! You too poor kill. Tell you what I do. I let you stay there t'ree day an' git fat, then I kills you!"

So the man made a cage and filled it full of feed. Buddah Rabbit took all the feed and mumbled it up making out he was eating.

Third day came, and Buddah Fox came along. Buddah Rabbit sneezed, "Whee, whee!"

Buddah Fox stopped, looked around. "Ain't I heard Buddah Rabbit?"

Buddah Rabbit sang out, "Yeah."

Buddah Fox asked, "Where?"

Buddah Rabbit said, "Right here in dis cage. Got good thing to eat! Keepin' me a store in here. Come on in. Don't bother 'bout de door. Come on in, Buddah Fox. All kinda good thing in here to eat."

After Buddah Fox went in, Buddah Rabbit decided he'd run and get him a drink of water. Buddah Fox busy eating.

Buddah Rabbit said, "I's be back directly."

Buddah Fox eating. Buddah Rabbit stayed away. Stayed away. Stayed away till it was time for him to be killed. Old man came. He asked, "Hey, Buddah Fox! What you doin' in there?"

"I's staying here for Buddah Rabbit while he gone to de spring."

Old man said, "Buddah Fox you ain't done nuttin'! I turn you out if you go on down an' carry message to Buddah Rabbit. Tell 'im if he don't come on back here an' git in dis cage, you goin' to eat 'im."

Buddah Fox agreed. The old man turned him out and he went on down the road and there he met Buddah Rabbit running. Buddah Rabbit running head down. Said Buddah Fox, "Dat a way for you to do!"

And Buddah Rabbit said, "I on my way now jest as hard as I kin go to turn you out."

Buddah Fox told him, "Old man seh I must tell you if you don't go back to dat cage, I must ketch you an' eat you!"

And Buddah Rabbit sang out, "Eat me! Don't eat me. I's too poor to eat. I show you where there's a old muddah goose and five head of goslin'. Eat dem fust, then you kin eat me. If you eat me fust, I can't show you de old muddah goose an' five head of goslin'."

So they slip! Slip, slip, slip! Till they came to a house. Then Buddah Rabbit showed Buddah Fox the nest of the mother goose and five head of gosling. Buddah Fox said he's going to ketch them all. And when he sprang he didn't land on any nest of goslings, he sprang on an old mother hound and five head of puppies. Old hound grabbed at Buddah Fox and she sang out, "Oh-oo! Oh-oo! Oh-oo!"

Trouble in the camp now. Fox running. Hound in behind him! "You! You! You! You!"

Buddah Rabbit jumped out the gate and got up on a big stump and called out, "E!E!E!E! Sick'em! E!E!E!E! Sick'em!"

Buddah Fox ran through the wood singing, "I do for you, Buddah Rabbit."

Buddah Rabbit sang out, "E!E!E!E! Sick'em! E!E!E!E! Sick'em! Do for me now Buddah Fox!"

Buddah Fox passed by another Buddah Fox and the other Buddah Fox called out, "Bear 'round. Bear 'round. Bear 'round." He didn't want those hounds to pick up *his* trail. Buddah Fox didn't have time to circle. Didn't have time to turn that day. Hound right in behind him.

And there was Buddah Rabbit sitting on the high stump clapping his hands and singing, "E!E!E!E! Sick'em! E!E!E!E! Sick'em!" "E!E!E!E! Sick'em! E!E!E!E! Sick'em!"

BETSEY LONG-TOOTH

One winter long ago in the north of England, an old man was walking a forest road. The traveler was hungry, threadbare and half frozen. In the gathering dusk a light ahead quickened his steps, until he stood before a snug thatched cottage. At his knock, the door was opened by an old woman who asked sharply, "Who are you and what do you want of Betsey Long-Tooth?" "I am a worn-out body known as Richard Woodward," he answered, "and I have walked long and far today without the blessing of a single crumb to break my fast. Surely I will die tonight, good mistress, if I am not preserved through the kindness of your heart."

"It is indeed too bitter a night," she answered, "for even a dog to have no shelter. Come in and warm your bones by the fire."

Closing the door, she followed him to the hearth, where a small fire licked at a steaming pot. The room was filled with the smell of good meat soup.

After the traveler had rested a little, the woman handed him an axe, saying, "If you want to eat supper, you must earn it. There is a woodpile in the rear and still enough light to work by."

The old man took the axe and stepped into the yard. Smoke from the chimney danced away on the raw east wind as he split several armloads of kindling. Then, daylight gone, he stacked the wood near the hearth and sat down close by the fire. While setting a rude oak table, the old woman told him her husband was dead and she had few kinsfolk. Her name came from the single long tooth left in her gums.

After they had eaten and the dishes had been cleared away, Betsey handed the old man a candle. Showing him to the door of a side room, she wished him a good night's sleep. He had catnapped on a feather mattress, under a pile of quilts, when he heard the hum of female voices. His curiosity got the best of him. Kneeling at the keyhole, he saw that several young women had joined Betsey; she was taking a bowl and some knitted wool nightcaps from a corner chest. Then she put the bowl on the hearth, and when its contents had melted she wet her fingers, annointed her head and clapped on a night cap.

"Gossip and gossip and up the chimney I go!" she said quite distinctly and disappeared, quick as a flash. Then the young women oiled their heads and put on nightcaps. Repeating the magic words, they vanished like their elder.

Richard Woodward now realized that his hostess was a witch. He threw on his clothes and hurried into the room so mysteriously left vacant. To his delight, a single nightcap lay on the floor, near the bowl which still contained a small amount of colorless liquid. Hesitantly he annointed his head, pulled the nightcap down to his ears and repeated, "Gossip and gossip and up the chimney I go!"

The next instant he found himself sitting on the chimney top. Betsey and the girls were perched on the roof's ridge. After a heated argument, the old witch finally said, "Gossip and gossip and to London Town I go!"

Each of the young women repeated the same words and disappeared into the night. Without further ado, Woodward said, "Gossip and gossip and to London Town I go!"

A short flight through icy air, and he floated gently down on a cobblestone street not far from London Bridge. The witches ignored his arrival and discussed their next move.

"We have come to the right place," said Betsey Long-Tooth. "I see a warehouse filled with fine cider. What say we celebrate the season right merrily?"

"Oh, let's do," chorused the young witches.

"Gossip and gossip and through the keyhole I go!" said Betsey, and through the keyhole she went. Her companions made haste to follow. A blast of wind howling down the snowy street made up Woodward's mind, and he too said, "Gossip and gossip and through the keyhole I go!"

The inside of the warehouse was pleasantly warm, and soon he could make out row upon row of stout oak casks. Like shadows the witches flitted, sampling the cider casks and then leaving their contents to trickle onto the floor.

"I might as well be hanged for a wolf as for a sheep," thought Woodward, so he too tasted the cider.

The witches frolicked until grey light stole up the river. Then Betsey whispered something to the girls. She left them laughing as she tightened the nightcap on her head and chanted, "Gossip and gossip and away home I go!"

One after another the witches disappeared, and little did Woodward notice the last to leave nabbed the cap from his head. "Gossip and gossip and away home I go!" he said, but instead of taking flight he banged his forehead on the keyhole and fell to the floor. Worn out with the night's unexpected events, he dozed off.

At sunup the owners of the warehouse arrived for another day's business. Finding their prize cider puddling on the floor and the old man in the corner, they lost no time in dragging him before a judge, where witnesses swore to their testimony.

"You know the penalty of the law for theft?" demanded the judge.

"Yes, milord," said Richard Woodward.

"Have you nothing at all to say in your defense before I pronounce judgement?"

"No, milord, nothing," said poor Richard, who feared the stake more than the gallows.

"Then tomorrow at sunrise you shall be led to Tyburn Hill and hanged by the neck until dead. And may God have mercy on your soul."

Richard Woodward was old, and he had already fought his bout with life. So with the courage of desperation, he resigned himself to leaving this world. But that night, in the cell where the jailor had securely locked him, he was roused by a hissing whisper.

"Richard, Richard Woodward, awake!" Surely he must have been dreaming—but then he heard footsteps at his side.

"Hurry, Richard, hurry. The sun will rise and the guards will take you to the gallows." It was Betsey Long-Tooth, come to save him from the hangman. Springing to his feet, he seized the bowl she offered, annointed his head and drew on a magic nightcap. Old Betsey adjusted her own cap and said, "Gossip and gossip and away home I go!"

"Gossip and gossip and away home I go," he echoed.

In the bat of an eye they were out of prison and over the river heading north. Soon they sighted the little cottage in the forest, flew down the chimney and landed side by side on the warm hearthstone.

"Let us marry," said Richard Woodward.

"I am willing," replied Betsey Long-Tooth.

And they lived merrily many years after.

CINDUH SEED IN YOU POCKET

Once there was a lil boy and he had some dogs.

How many dogs? You jes' wait and count 'em.

And the lil boy's mama put some cinduh seed in his pocket.

Cinduh seed? Why, they was jes' cinduh seed. They grown on top of the cinduh sallet in the garden jes' like must'ed and turnip sallet.

And the lil boy's mama put some of the cinduh seed in his pocket and tole him if he got into trouble, to th'ow the cinduh seed outen his pocket, and that'll git him out of the trouble.

And the lil boy went on 'bout his business and clean forgot the cinduh seed in his pocket.

And not long after that, the lil boy went way off from home in a country where they didn't like him, and some men tuck out after him to git him. They runned after him a long way till he come to a tree, and he climb the tree, and kept on going up higher and higher.

Then the men went and fetched axes and began to chop the tree down, and the lil boy he got nearly scairt to deff when he seed the chips a-flyin'.

All to oncet he recollek what his mama tole him 'bout the cinduh seed. And he felt in his pocket, and there they was! So he tuck a few and th'owed 'em on the men a-cuttin' on the tree, and all to oncet the chips flewed back where they come from and mended up the tree.

And the lil boy kept sayin' over and over, "Drop down, my cinduh seed, mend up my good tree. Mend up, mend up."

And fast as the men cut 'em out, the chips'd fly back into place and mend up the tree like it was fo' the lil boy climb it.

And the lil boy thought 'bout his dogs he had left at home, and he begin saying to himself:

Hi, Bark and Berry,
Jupiter and Kerry,
Darker-in-de-mawnin'!
Why don't chu come along?

Then he begin to call the dogs out loud, while the axes made the chips fly, and he dropped cinduh seed, and they made the chips fly back into the tree.

Come on, Bark and Berry,
Jupiter and Kerry,
Darker-in-de-mawnin'!
Come on-n-n, on, on!
Come on! Come on!

And jes' as the lil boy was dropping his last cinduh seed, here come his dogs, and they jes' flewed into them men what was chopping down the tree and et 'em up, head and feet. That's what Bark done, and what Berry and Kerry and Darker-in-de-mawnin' all done.

And the lil boy went on back home, and his dogs galloped at his heels.

How many dogs? Didn't I count 'em?

Well, ever one of 'em was chock full of choppers they had et.

HOW THE DEER GOT
HIS HORNS

In the beginning the Deer had no horns, but his head was smooth just like a doe's. He was a great runner and the Rabbit was a great jumper, and the animals were all curious to know which could go farther in the same time. They talked about it a good deal, and at last arranged a match between the two, and made a nice large pair of antlers for a prize to the winner. They were to start together from

one side of a thicket and go through it, then turn and come back, and the one who came out first was to get the horns.

On the day fixed all the animals were there, with the antlers put down on the ground at the edge of the thicket to mark the starting point. While everybody was admiring the horns the Rabbit said: "I don't know this part of the country; I want to take a look through the bushes where I am to run." They thought that all right, so the Rabbit went into the thicket, but he was gone so long that at last the animals suspected he must be up to one of his tricks. They sent a messenger to look for him, and away in the middle of the thicket he found the Rabbit gnawing down the bushes and pulling them away until he had a road cleared to the other side.

The messenger turned around quietly and came back and told the other animals. When the Rabbit came out at last they accused him of cheating, but he denied it until they went into the thicket and found the cleared road. They agreed that such a trickster had no right to enter the race at all, so they gave the horns to the Deer, who was admitted to be the best runner, and he has worn them ever since. They told the Rabbit that as he was so fond of cutting down bushes he might do that for a living hereafter, and so he does to this day.

A LOAD OF
WATERMELON

There was an old lady by the name of Nancy, and she had an acre of watermelon. And there was an old man by the name of Joe, and he loved watermelon very much. So he said to her, "Mis' Nancy, dear, if I go and spen' a night in that old haunted house, will you give me a load of watermelon?"

"Oh, with all my heart," replied Mis' Nancy.

"You lose a load of watermelon," said Uncle Joe.

So that night Uncle Joe went to the haunted house. He was a man who did not believe in ghosts. At midnight he was sitting by the fire, thinking how he was going to eat watermelon and how he was going to sell some.

About half-past twelve up jumped a ghost and sat beside him, and said, "Oh just we two!"

Uncle Joe's eyes grew big and the hair on his head rose up and he said, "Won't be but one in a minute."

Through the window he went and took half the window along with him. He ran and ran until he'd run six miles, then he saw a rabbit going along the road. He said to the rabbit, "Get out of the way! Get out of the way! Let someone run who can run!"

He ran until he ran right into a willow tree and knocked himself almost dead. People found him the next morning and took him to his house. When he could talk he said, "Tell Mis' Nancy she can have her watermelon!"

And if you want to fight, ask Uncle Joe if there're ghosts in the world.

He step on a pin, an' the pin ben',
An' now my story is end.

DING, A-DING, DING

The king had a fine daughter. Buh Rabbit asked the king for his daughter and the king said, "If you git me one bag o' blackbird, one rattlesnake tooth an' one alligatuh tooth, you will hab my daughtah."

So Buh Rabbit went down the road singing,

Ding, ding, ding, a-ding, ding, ding,

Ding-a ding, ding, ding.

He saw some blackbirds in a field, so he took a bag and said, "Hey, you blackbird, up deh singin' so big, I bet you can't full dis bag."

The blackbirds flew in the bag and Buh Rabbit tied the string and took the bag to the king. The king told him, "You a smart man, Buh Rabbit. Now git me de rattlesnake tooth."

Buh Rabbit met Buh Rattlesnake. Said, "Good mornin', Buh Rattlesnake. You sho' is growin' mighty big. Let me measure you wid dis stick to see how long you is." Buh Rattlesnake lay down long side the stick and Buh Rabbit tied his tail to the stick.

"What for you tie my tail, Buh Rabbit?"

"Oh, man, I have to tie you' tail to straight you out so's I can measure you good." Then he tied the rattlesnakes's head and pulled the string tight and choked him to death. He took out a tooth and carried it to the king. King said, "Buh Rabbit, you *too* smart. Now bring me de alligatuh tooth."

Buh Rabbit went down to the point and found the alligator and called out, "Oh Buh Gatuh, come up here on de shore. Gwine hab big time up here." Gator came up.

Buh Rabbit said, "Now we play a little game." And he sang,

Go t'rough my legs swif'ly, O,
An' come back slowly, O.

Buh Gator went through swiftly and when he came back slowly, Buh Rabbit knocked him with a stick. The gator pitched into the pond saying, "Buh Rabbit, you *too* mean."

Buh Rabbit studied how he could get Buh Gator to come out again. Finally he went off and killed a squirrel and dressed up in the squirrel's clothes. He came back to the pond singing,

Ding ding, ding, a-ding, ding, ding, ding,

Ding, ding-a ding, ding.

Buh Gator said, "I t'ink I hear Buh Rabbit voice."

Buh Rabbit said, "Come on up Buh Gatuh. It's me, Buh Squirrel."

Gator's wife told him, "Don't go up there, you might git hurt."

Gator called out, "Dat you, Buh Squirrel?"

"Yeah, come on up."

Buh Gator came up on shore. He said, "Dat Buh Rabbit a *mean* man. He knocked me wid a stick. But I glad he didn't hit me on *dis* side, 'cause I would-a been daid."

So Buh Rabbit took a stick and hit him on that side and knocked him dead. Then he pulled out a tooth and took it to the king.

The king told him, "Man, you *too* smart."

Buh Rabbit said, "Eider gib me yo' daughtah or gib me trouble."

The king said, "I'll gib you trouble."

So he gave Buh Rabbit a bag and told him, "Don't open um till you come to a wide field."

Buh Rabbit went off to a wide field and undid the bag. Out jumped three hound dogs right after Buh Rabbit. One of the dogs bit off Buh Rabbit's tail, and his tail's been short to this day.

BUDDAH RABBIT
AND THE MUSIC MAN

Yes sir! Buddah Rabbit's into everything. One time Buddah Rabbit played a trick on Buddah Gator.

Now Buddah Gator, he's the fiddler, the music man. All the gals were stuck on Buddah Gator. Buddah Gator thought *every* day was good. They had a dance, Buddah Gator calling,
Hands away

Balansay!
Hug me darlin'
Turn your contrary partner,
And your partner at home!
Such a time they had! Buddah Gator had a steady time. He said,
Every day good!
Every day good!
Every day good!
He had no trouble in his life. The gals turned and turned. No change in the music. No turning in the music.

Buddah Rabbit said, "Buddah Gator, I fiddle a little and rest you. You dance a while." Taking the fiddle, he jumped up, calling,
Turn your contrary partner
Remember your partner at home!
Then Buddah Rabbit played,
Some day good!
Some day bad!
Some day good!
Some day bad!
That music suit 'em. Suit 'em so good.
Some day good!
Some day bad!
Some day good!
Some day bad!
Buddah Rabbit fiddled off that piece.

Buddah Gator didn't like that as well. Buddah Rabbit beat him at the fiddling. Gals danced so good, so good to Buddah Rabbit's music.

Buddah Gator and Buddah Rabbit were talking. Buddah Gator said, "TROUBLE? What is TROUBLE? I never see TROUBLE in my life."

Now one day, more than ever, tide came up in stormy weather. Blew up a lot of dead marsh. Dead marsh grass on the bank! Buddah Gator crawled out there in the sunshine on that dry marsh grass and went to sleep. Buddah Rabbit walked round and round. Round and round Buddah Gator Buddah Rabbit walked, and all the time he was stringing fire on the dead marsh grass, just a-stringing fire round Buddah Gator.

When he got all around Buddah Gator, Buddah Rabbit yelled out, TROUBLE, TROUBLE, TROUBLE, Buddah Gator."

Buddah Gator opened his eye. Fire coming at him. Getting hotter and hotter. He raised up and hollered, "BOO-JOO, BOO-JOO."

He went over in the river. Over in the river out of the fire.

Buddah Rabbit said, "Buddah Gator, I tell you dey *is* trouble! I been tellin' you 'bout trouble!"

Some day good.

Some day bad.

All day ain't good!

And Buddah Gator acknowledged there was TROUBLE in the world.

THE TAILFISHER

The rabbit met the fox carryin' a long string of fish. "Where did you get all them fish, Mr. Fox?"

The fox carried the rabbit down to a hole in the ice an' told him to sit over it all night with his tail hanging down in the water, an' in the morning he'd have a nice string of fish on his tail.

But in the morning the rabbit's tail was froze in the ice. The rabbit

77

pulled an' pulled but he couldn't get loose.

    The owl came an' pulled him first by one ear and then by th' other, but rabbit's ears jus' stretched out long, an' he still stuck. Finally they got him loose, but his tail pulled off an' stuck in the ice. That's how come the rabbit has sech long ears an' sech a short tail.

SEVEN BLUE
BUTTERFLIES

There was a little old boy long time ago, didn't have no mammy or poppy, jest growed up in the hog weeds, and he didn't even know his name, but everybody called him Jack. And he jest stayed here and yonder, wherever he could drop in at night.

So one day he was a walkin' the road, and he had him a belt around his waist and he had him a little old knife, and he was a whitlin' and makin' him a paddle. So he come along past a mud hole, and there was a lot of little old blue butterflies over hit. So he struck down with his paddle and he killed seven of the butterflies. So he goes on a little piece further and he comes to a blacksmith shop, and he gets the blacksmith to cut letters in his belt, "Stiff Dick killed seven at a lick."

So he goes on a piece further and he passes the king's house. King runs out and says, "I see you're a very brave man; I see where you've killed seven at a lick."

"Yes, bedads, I'm a mighty brave man."

So the king says, "Stranger, I want to hire a brave man to kill some animals we have here in the woods. We have a wild municorn here killin' so many people, soon we'll all be kilt. If you'll kill that municorn, we'll pay you one thousand dollars, five hundred down, and five hundred when you bring the municorn in."

So Dick says, "All right."

So the king paid him five hundred dollars. Stiff Dick stuck that in his pocket and said to hisself, "Bedads, if they ever see me around here again." And he tuk out.

When he got way up in the mountains the municorn smelled him and here it come,

Whippity cut,

Whippity cut,

Whippity cut.

Stiff Dick tuk to runnin' and the municorn after him. The municorn was jest clippin' Stiff Dick. They run up the mountains and down the ridges. So long late in the evening they started down a long ridge, the municorn jest a runnin' after Stiff Dick. And away down at the end of the ridge Stiff Dick saw a big oak and he made a

beeline to see if he cud clumb hit. So the municorn was jest a gettin' so close that agin they got there the municorn was jest behin' him. Jack jest slipped around the oak right quick and the municorn stove his horn into hit and he just rared and plunged.

As soon as Stiff Dick saw he was fastened for all time to come, he went on to the king's house. King says, "Did you get the municorn?"

Dick says, "Municorn? Laws an massy, never was nothin' but little old bull calf come tearin' out there after me. I jest picked it up by one ear and tail and stove it agin a tree and if you all wanst hit, you'll have to go up thar and git hit."

So the king got him a great army and went up and killed the municorn, come back and paid Jack five hundred dollars more. King says, "Now, Stiff Dick, there's one more wild animal living up here, a wild bull-boar. I'll give five hundred dollars now and five hundred more when you ketch hit."

Jack tuk the five hundred dollars and says to hisself, "You'll never see me anymore." But after he'd gone a little ways here come the wild boar after him,

Whippity cut,

Whippity cut,

Whippity cut.

All day long around the mountains, across the mountains and down the ridges, all the day just a runnin'. So along late in the evenin' away down in the holler he saw an old house and when he got down there the door was open. So he run right in the door and up the wall and the wild boar run right after him and laid down under him. Boar was tired and soon fell asleep. So Dick eased up the wall and over and down the outside and shut the wild boar up in there.

So he went down to the king's house. King says, "Did ye git the wild boar?"

Stiff Dick says, "Wild boar? Laws a massy, I never saw nothing but a little old boar pig come bristlin' up after me. I jest picked hit up by the tail and throwed hit in an old waste house. And if you all wanst hit, you'll have to go up thar and git hit."

So king got up an army of men and went up and killed the wild boar and went back down and paid Stiff Dick his other five hundred dollars. King says, "Now, Stiff Dick, there's one more wild animal we want to git killed. That's a big brown bear." So he give Dick another five hundred dollars.

Stiff Dick says to hisself, "If I can jest get out of here no brown bear 'ul never see me." So he got way up on the mountain; old brown bear smelled him and here he come,

Whippity cut,
Whippity cut,
Whippity cut.

Across the hills, up the ridges, every way to dodge the bear. The bear uz right after him. So late in the evenin', way down at the end of a ridge he saw an old pine tree that had been all burned over and was right black. Jack made a beeline fur that tree. Bear was jest a little ways behind when Jack run up the tree. Bear was down at the root of the tree and he was so mad he tried to gnaw the tree down. Hit gnawed and gnawed. Jack keep a easin' down on another old snag and another old snag and directly he got on a snag jest above the old bear and the old snag broke and Jack fell just a straddle the old bear, and they jest burnt the wind.

Stiff Dick was so tickled and so scared, too, that he was jest a hollerin' and screamin and directly he run the bear right thru the

83

town and the soldier boys heared him a-screamin' and they run out and shot hit. Stiff Dick got off it when it fell, and he was jest a swearin' and a rarin'. He was swearin' he was breakin' hit for the king a riddy horse. And king come out and heard Stiff Dick a swearin' he was a breakin' the bear for the king a riddy house and he got mad and made the soldier boys pay Dick five hundred dollars.

And when I left there Stiff Dick was rich.

ABOUT THE TALES

The three major groups of folk tradition found in the Carolinas, in the order of their coming to this area, are Indian, British and black. The last was chiefly from the Bahamas and West Africa.

Most of the Indian stories in this book are Cherokee. Part of this tribe still lives on the Cherokee Reservation in the Great Smoky Mountains and here is represented by the animal tales collected by James Mooney: "How the Rabbit Stole the Otter's Coat," "Why the

Possum's Tail Is Bare," "How the Deer Got his Horns," and "The Ball Game of the Birds and Animals." There are also three short Catawba tales which came from their former chief, Sam Blue, who in the 1940s headed a remnant of the tribe living south of Rock Hill.

Of the British tales, "Seven Blue Butterflies" belongs to the group of Old Jack, Will and Tom tales found in the Southern Blue Ridge. It is given in the words of Mrs. Jane Gentry of Hot Springs (north of Asheville) who heard it from her grandfather, and its Elizabethan phrases are used even today by isolated mountaineers. "Pappy's Tater Patch" was told by E. R. Hawkins, a potato farmer of McDowell County, North Carolina in the shadow of Mount Mitchell, where there are many knobs, usually of no value for crops. "Betsey Long-Tooth"—surely someone's memory of an English tale—was reported by Hugh Buckner Johnson of Wilson County, North Carolina. "The Tailfisher" came from W. L. Pierce of nearby Edge-combe County, and "The Enchanted Cloak" is from old Charleston.

The largest group of tales in this book are from black storytellers. Of those gathered in North Carolina, "The Whang Doodle" was told by Alex White of Polk County, just east of Hendersonville, who claimed that the experience with the Whang Doodle occurred on his father's farm when he was a boy. "Cinduh Seed In You Pocket" was told by Evelyn Franklin Robbins, a schoolteacher, who believed it came from Madison, north of Greensboro.

The rest of the tales are from coastal South Carolina and were recorded in varying versions of Gullah. This dialect is discussed by Guy Johnson in his "Folk Culture on St. Helena Island, South Carolina." Dr. Johnson found the most numerous class in the early days of the colony to be of English peasant stock, indentured servants, laborers and artisans, who spoke dialect as distinguished from literary English. It was this group which later worked closely as overseers with the blacks and taught them a basic English, with simplified tenses, inflection, gender and number. Gullah, suggests Dr. Johnson, was probably a shortened form of Angola, a district on the west coast of Africa, near the Congo's mouth, or from a Liberian group of tribes known as Golas, living between Sierra Leone and the Ivory Coast.

The average reader today has difficulty understanding Gullah, and so it seemed best to omit or modify much of the dialect, so that the tales could still be enjoyed. "Addie's Plat-Eye," contributed by Genevieve Willcox Chandler, probably came from the Beaufort area. The plat-eye is a form of spirit known to lure its victims away, and especially fond of losing them in woods.

"The Rabbit, Fox and Goose" and "Buddah Rabbit and the Music Man" came from near Murrell's Inlet. "Who Stole Buh Kinlaw's Goat?" has a verse opening common on Ladies Island, a type of introduction used also in the Bahamas. "Ding A-Ding, Ding" was told by James Henderson at Eddings' Point School on St. Helena Island. These two are also from Beaufort County, South Carolina. "The Talking Mule" was told by Jack Brown, a native of Daufuskie Island, and here the verse is at the end. "A Load of Watermelon" was told by Nellie Dudley, a pupil at Penn School, St. Helena. These tales from the sea islands are all from near Beaufort.

ACKNOWLEDGMENTS

For permission to reprint, adapt or retell the stories listed below, the editor is indebted to:

THE AMERICAN FOLKLORE SOCIETY, for the following:

From the *Journal of American Folklore:*

"Seven Blue Butterflies," formerly "Old Stiff Dick" from *Mountain White Folk-lore: Tales of the Southern Blue Ridge,* recorded by Isabel Gordon Carter, Vol. XXXVIII (1925); "The Tailfisher," from *North Carolina Folktales and Riddles,* recorded by Ralph Steele Boggs, Vol. XLVII (Oct.-Dec. 1934); "A Spider Helper," a retelling of "A Spider Helper"; "Rooster in the Tree," a retelling of "Rooster and Fox"; and "A Hop-Toad in a Gourd," a retelling of "The Smart Man"; from *Catawba Folk Tales* recorded by F. G. Speck and L. G. Carr, Vol. LX (1947).

From the *Memoirs of the American Folklore Society:*

"The Talking Mule," a retelling of No. 61, "The Talking Mule"; and "A Load of Watermelon," a retelling of No. 62, Version IV of "Racing a Ghost"; from *Folklore of the Sea Islands, South Carolina,* by Elsie Clews Parsons, Vol. XVI (1923).

JOHN BENNETT JR., for "The Enchanted Cloak" from "Folktales from Old Charleston," recorded by John Bennett in *The Yale Review,* Vol. XXXII (1943). Used by permission of John Bennett Jr.

DUKE UNIVERSITY PRESS, for the following:

"Cinduh Seed In You Pocket," "Pappy's Tater Patch" and "The Whang Doodle" in *Bundle of Troubles and Other Tarheel Tales,* ed. by W. C. Hendricks, Duke University Press, 1943, 1971. Used by permission of Duke University Press.

"Betsey Long-Tooth," a retelling of "Betsey Long-Tooth," recorded by Dr. A. P. Hudson in *The Frank C. Brown Collection of North Carolina Folklore,* Vol. I. ed. by Newman Ivey White. Duke University Press, 1952. Used and retold by permission of Duke University Press.

SMITHSONIAN INSTITUTION PRESS, for the following:
"How The Rabbit Stole The Otter's Coat," "Why the Possum's Tail Is Bare," "How The Deer Got His Horns," "The Ball Game of the Birds and Animals," from "Myths Of The Cherokee" by James Mooney in *The 19th Annual Report of the Bureau of American Ethnology,* 1897-98, Part I, 1900. Used by permission of the Smithsonian Institution Press.

UNIVERSITY OF NORTH CAROLINA PRESS, for the following:
"Who Stole Buh Kinlaw's Goat?," a retelling of the same title and "Ding, A-Ding, Ding," a retelling of "Rabbit Seeks a Wife," from *Folk Culture On St. Helena Island, South Carolina* by Guy B. Johnson, University of North Carolina Press, 1930. Used by permission of the University of North Carolina Press.

UNIVERSITY OF SOUTH CAROLINA, for the following:
"Addie's Plat-Eye," a retelling of "Ad's Plat-Eye"; "Buddah Rabbit and the Music Man," a retelling of "Buddah Rabbit and Buddah Gatah"; and "The Rabbit, Fox and Goose," a retelling of "Buh Rabbit, Fox and Goose"; in *South Carolina Folk Tales,* Louise Jones Dubose, ed., Bulletin of the University of South Carolina, 1941.